A NOTE TO PARENTS

Disney's **First Readers Level 1** books were developed with the beginning reader in mind. They feature large, easy-to-read type, lots of repetition, and simple vocabulary.

One of the most important ways parents can help their child develop a love of reading is by providing an *environment* for reading. Every time you discuss a book, read aloud to your child, or your child observes you reading, you promote the development of early reading skills and habits. Here are some tips to help you use **Disney's First Readers Level 1** books with your child:

★ Tell the story about the original Disney film or video. Storytelling is crucial to language development. A young child needs a language *foundation* before reading skills can begin to emerge.

★ Talk about the illustrations in the book. Beginning readers need to use illustrations to gather clues about unknown words or to understand the story.

★ Read aloud to your child. When you read aloud, run your finger smoothly under the text. Do not stop at each word. Enliven the text for your child by using a different voice for each character. In other words, be an actor—and have fun!

★ "Read it again!" Children love hearing stories read again and again. When they begin reading on their own, repetition helps them feel successful. Maintain patience, be encouraging, and expect to read the same books over and over.

★ Play "question and answer." Use the After-Reading Fun activities provided at the end of each book to further enhance your child's learning process.

Remember that early-reading experiences that you share with your child can help him or her to become a confident and successful reader later on!

— Patricia Koppman
Past President
International Reading Association

Where's Oddball?

by Mary Hogan
Designed by Paul W. Banks

Disney's First Readers — Level 1
A Story from Disney's *102 Dalmatians*

SCHOLASTIC INC.

New York   Toronto   London   Auckland   Sydney
Mexico City   New Delhi   Hong Kong   Buenos Aires

Little Dipper and Domino
are looking for Oddball.

Where is that pup?

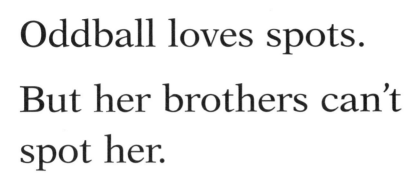

Oddball loves spots.

But her brothers can't spot her.

Domino meets Chomp.

"Where is Oddball?"
asks Domino.

Chomp saw Oddball
a moment ago.

But he does not
see her now.

Little Dipper meets Drooler.

He asks, "Do you know where Oddball is?"

Drooler does not.

Domino meets Digger.

"Is Oddball here?"
asks Domino.

Digger shakes
his head.

Little Dipper and Domino meet Fluffy.

"Have you seen Oddball?" ask Little Dipper and Domino.

Fluffy has not.

How will Little Dipper
and Domino find Oddball?

Domino has a plan.

Little Dipper and Domino
lay out a trail of treats.

They wait for Oddball
to find them!

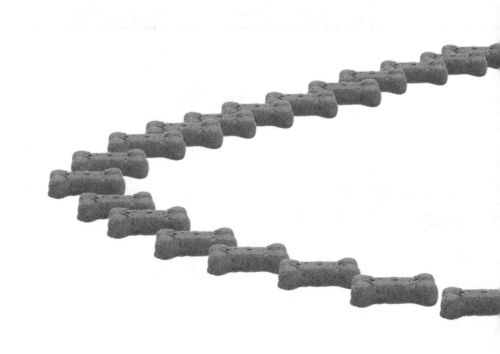

They wait for a long time,
then they hear. . . .

CRUNCH-CRUNCH-CRUNCH.

Here comes Chomp.

Chomp and the pups wait
for Oddball. They hear. . .

CRUNCH - slurp~slurp.

Here comes Drooler.

Now four dogs wait for Oddball. They hear. . .

CRUNCH-**MUNCH-MUNCH.**

Here comes Digger.

Five dogs wait for Oddball.
They hear a small sound. . .

CRUNCH-CRUNCH-CRUNCH.

Here comes Fluffy.

"Where can Oddball be?"
asks Digger.

Fluffy looks at the treats.

"I've spotted the problem," he says.

The dogs lay out a new
trail of treats.

They wait for Oddball
to find them.

CRUNCH-CRUNCH-CRUNCH.

"SURPRISE!"

"I found you!"
says Oddball.

Woof!

Enhance the reading experience with follow-up questions to help your child develop reading comprehension and increase his/her awareness of words.

Approach this with a sense of play. Make a game of having your child answer the questions. You do not need to ask all the questions at one time. Let these questions be fun discussions rather than a test. If your child doesn't have instant recall, encourage him/her to look back into the book to "research" the answers. You'll be modeling what good readers do and, at the same time, forging a sharing bond with your child.

Where's Oddball?

1. Who were the dogs looking for in the story?

2. Name some places where Oddball hid.

3. How did the puppies try to get Oddball to come to them?

4. Whose idea was it to make a line of dog biscuits?

5. Which dogs waited for Oddball to arrive?

6. Where is your favorite hiding place?

Answers: 1. Oddball. 2. behind a ball, behind presents, in a doghouse, behind a cone, behind a garbage can, behind a window. 3. they line up dog biscuits. 4. Domino's. 5. Little Dipper, Domino, Chomp, Drooler, Digger, and Fluffy. 6. answers will vary.